The artist wishes to thank
Ben Parker, Zoe and Luccombe Dalmatians

ISBN 1 85854 535 8
Published by Brimax Books Ltd, Newmarket,
England, CB8 7AU 1997.
Printed in China.

Smutter!

by VINCE MARSDEN

Illustrated by SUSAN NEALE

Smutter is my puppy.
He is black and white. Everyone says he is full of mischief.

On Sunday...

Smutter sat under the kitchen table, gnawing at a big bone. He was really enjoying crunching through the hard layer and licking away at the soft marrow inside.

"Crunch, munch, lick, lick," says Smutter.

The only problem was...

Mother soon realised the meat for Sunday dinner was missing. She was very angry and chased Smutter with her wooden spoon.

On Monday...

Smutter found some cuddly toys.
A yellow giraffe, a brown teddy bear and an orange elephant.
Smutter loved those toys. He dragged them all around the house,
shaking and throwing his head, until the toys were torn right open.
Then he snuggled down on top of the stuffing and went to sleep.

The only problem was...

The cuddly toys belonged to my little sister.
She loved the yellow giraffe, the brown teddy bear and the orange
elephant. When she saw what Smutter had done, she cried and
cried and cried!

On Tuesday...

Smutter caught a snake in our back yard. It was slithering
along by the shed. Smutter was very brave. First he yapped, then
he jumped backwards a little before leaping on top of the snake.
The snake was massive! I couldn't even see its tail!
Smutter pounced. He grabbed the snake and rolled around,
twisting and coiling, wrapping and writhing. Eventually,
Smutter succeeded in killing the snake.

The only problem was...

When Uncle Tom borrowed my father's hose to wash his car!

On Wednesday...

Smutter found a new friend - Pickles. Pickles and Smutter got
along really well. First they played chase. Smutter chased Pickles
all around our yard. When he caught her - he bit her tail!
They played at pretend boxing. Pickles got a little carried away
and punched poor Smutter right on the nose!
In the end they played hide and seek but Smutter wasn't very
good at seeking. He spent the rest of the day sitting right
beneath the apple tree without realising that Pickles was hiding
right above his head.

The only problem was...

Mrs Jones from next door really did worry too much about her prize winning Persian cat.

On Thursday...

Smutter was in the garden. I found him frantically digging
where Grandpa was growing his plants. It looked as though he
had found something really interesting, but in the end it turned
out to be a smelly old dinosaur bone. Smutter must have felt
very proud though. He scurried into the house to find a quiet
corner to study his find.

The only problem was...

When Mother saw the muddy paw prints on the carpet she went mad. She shouted at Smutter and chased him with her wooden spoon again.

On Friday...

Smutter and I went for a walk in the park. He was as good as gold! When I went for an ice-cream cone Smutter waited for me by the old clock tower. It wasn't Smutter that chased the ducks away from the pond! It wasn't Smutter that interrupted the soccer match by running off with the corner flag! It wasn't Smutter that pinched the balls from the tennis courts and buried them behind the swings and it certainly wasn't Smutter that trampled down all the flower beds!

The only problem was...

When the park manager knocked at our front door, Smutter ran
upstairs and hid under my bed. I suddenly became very suspicious.

On Saturday...

Mother declared that she was at the end of her tether! Grandpa said, well, Grandpa didn't say much at all because Smutter had buried his false teeth. My little sister was still crying over her toys. Finally, Father said that the dog would have to go - the very next day!

I was heartbroken. Smutter was my dog.
"Why are grown ups always so cruel?" I kept asking myself.

Mind you...

That was nearly seven years ago and Smutter is still here.
We're both a bit older now and much wiser. Smutter is
still as mischievous as ever and is always in trouble for it!
But we love him more than ever.